MYTHOLOGY OF THE WORLD

GODDESSES OF WORLD MYTHOLOGY

by Rachel Bithell

BrightPoint Press

San Diego, CA

an imprint of ReferencePoint Press, Inc.
Printed in the United States

For more information, contact:
BrightPoint Press
PO Box 27779
San Diego, CA 92198
www.BrightPointPress.com

LIBRARY OF CONGRESS CATALOGING-IN-PUBLICATION DATA

Name: Bithell, Rachel, author.
Title: Goddesses of World Mythology / by Rachel Bithell.
Description: San Diego, CA: BrightPoint Press, 2023 | Series: Mythology of the World | Includes bibliographical references and index. | Audience: Grades 7–9
Identifiers: ISBN 9781678204945 (hardcover) | ISBN 9781678204952 (eBook)
The complete Library of Congress record is available at www.loc.gov.

CONTENTS

AT A GLANCE

- Goddesses were important in the mythology of many cultures. The divine beings in the earliest stories were likely female.
- Goddesses played central roles in many creation myths. These are stories about how the world, parts of nature, and humans came to be.
- In many of these myths, parts of the world were made from a goddess's body.
- Many ancient people appealed to goddesses for easy and safe childbirth.
- Goddesses were also believed to help and protect mothers and children.
- Some cultures connected goddesses to death and the afterlife. Some of these goddesses were cruel, while others were merciful.

- Many myths tell of goddesses giving gifts or blessings. These gifts might help just one person or the whole world.
- Stories of goddesses from the past still influence modern cultures.

INTRODUCTION

TIAMAT AND MARDUK

In the beginning, Tiamat and Apsu lived alone in peace. Tiamat was the goddess of **chaos** and salt water. Her husband, Apsu, was the god of fresh water. Soon they had children and then grandchildren. These younger gods were rude and noisy. Apsu decided to kill them. One of the couple's sons learned of the plan and killed Apsu.

Tiamat was furious. She took the form of a serpent and attacked the younger gods. They asked the warrior Marduk to defend

Marduk used Tiamat's body parts to make features of the world. Her eyes became rivers, and her breasts became mountains.

Gods who looked more like humans eventually replaced nature gods in mythology. Some of the earliest deities were goddesses.

them. He was known to be both fierce and wise. The other gods agreed to make Marduk their king if he won. He caught Tiamat in his net. She opened her mouth to swallow him. But he blew a gale that stretched her belly like a balloon. He then shot an arrow into her heart. With his sword, he split Tiamat's body in two. One half became the sky. The other half became the earth. With Tiamat and Apsu out of the way, Marduk became the most powerful of the gods.

MYTHS AND GODDESSES

This myth comes from ancient Babylon. Like many myths, it explains the creation of part of the world. It tells how a goddess became the sky and the earth. This myth also represents an important change.

Gods were usually the more powerful deities in later myths. But goddesses continued to play key roles in world mythology.

It comes from a time when ancient Babylonians stopped worshipping older **deities**. These older gods were like forces of nature. Instead, the Babylonians turned to younger gods who were more like humans.

A similar change occurred in other cultures. Often, this happened before a culture had a written language. Stories about this change became part of the cultures' myths.

The older stories featured goddesses who were as vital as the gods. In many cases, the goddesses were even more powerful than the gods. In fact, experts think the earliest deities in mythology were female. In later belief systems, male gods were usually in charge. However, goddesses remained important in world mythology.

1

GODDESSES OF CREATION

Goddesses were important in many creation stories. As with Tiamat, creation myths sometimes began in a watery chaos. Another example is the story of Luonnotar (LOH-nuh-tahr) from Finland. In the beginning of time, she was the only being. In 1835, the poet Elias Lönnrot wrote about this goddess of the air. He wrote, "Her existence [was] sad and hopeless, thus alone to live for ages."[1]

Finally, a duck flew over, looking for a nesting place. When Luonnotar raised her knee out of the water, the duck landed on it. The bird built a nest and laid seven eggs.

For a while, the Finnish goddess Luonnotar was the only being. She then helped create the sun, the moon, and the rest of the world.

The eggs grew hot. Soon, the heat burned Luonnotar. She shook the nest from her knee. This caused the eggs to shatter. The earth and sky formed from pieces of the shells. The moon was made from the egg whites. The sun came from the yellow yolks. Luonnotar saw the beauty of the world. She then formed all the other features of the land and ocean.

CREATING NATURE AND OTHER GODS

In many myths, nature forms from a goddess's own body. Tiamat's body becoming the earth and the sky is an example. Ancient people saw that a woman's body created babies. This may have led to stories about the body of a goddess becoming parts of the natural world. Sometimes, as with Tiamat, the goddess is killed or injured.

OFFERINGS AND SACRIFICES

Ancient people often made offerings to goddesses. They wanted to ask for favors or avoid punishment. Offerings could include food, jewelry, wine, oil, or **incense**. Sometimes animals were sacrificed as offerings. The Aztecs believed the goddess Tlaltecuhtli wanted human sacrifices. Some other cultures, such as the Inca and Assyrians, also sacrificed people.

The Aztec deity Tlaltecuhtli could appear as either male or female. She is shown here as a woman.

A similar fate befell the fierce Aztec goddess Tlaltecuhtli (TLAHL-tuh-KOOT-lee). She had extra mouths on her elbows and knees. They often snapped open, hungry for blood. Two powerful gods wanted to create a world. But they didn't want Tlaltecuhtli in it. They decided to kill her. The gods turned themselves into snakes. Then they grabbed Tlaltecuhtli by her hands and feet. Pulling with godly strength, they tore her in half. They made the sky with one half of her body. They made the earth with the other. Her skin and hair became grasses and flowers. Her eyes and mouth became caves, wells, and rivers. Her nose and shoulders became valleys and mountains. Her body was transformed. But her angry spirit lived on. Sometimes it could be heard in earthquakes or volcanoes.

Ra tried to keep the Egyptian goddess Nut from having children. But Thoth helped her find a way around Ra's curse.

Often, goddesses created other gods. Many goddesses had children and grandchildren. They became new deities. The Egyptian goddess Nut also created parts of nature and a new family of gods.

Nut was the granddaughter of Ra, the great sun god of Egypt. She married her brother Geb. Egyptian gods and goddesses often married close relatives. Siblings who marry each other also appear in myths from around the world.

Geb and Nut held each other very tightly. Nothing could come between them. Ra ordered their father, Shu, to separate them. As the god of air, Shu blew a mighty wind. It lifted Nut to become the sky. Geb became the earth. People could now live in the space between them. Ra placed stars on Nut to make her beautiful.

Nut wished to have children. Ra was afraid a great-grandchild would steal his throne. One version of this story comes from the ancient Greek philosopher Plutarch. He recorded it around 100 CE. He said, "The Sun [Ra] . . . invoked a curse upon her that she should not give birth to a child in any month or year."[2] Nut was heartbroken. She asked Thoth, the god of wisdom, for help. He challenged the moon to a board game similar to checkers. If Thoth won, some moonlight would be his prize. Thoth won easily. He used the moonlight to add five extra days to the end of the year. Nut could have children on the new days. She gave birth to Osiris, Horus, Seth, Isis, and Nephthys (NEF-this).

CREATING HUMANS

Some cultures had myths about goddesses creating humans. The story of Nuwa from China is one example. After the world was

NATURE SPIRITS

The Greek nymphs were minor goddesses of nature. They guarded trees, meadows, mountains, and water. In some European myths, nature spirits could be male or female. They could also be kind or cruel. The Slavic rusalki were female spirits who tried to drown men.

The Chinese goddess Nuwa sometimes appears as a human. But many images show her with a woman's head and a snake's body.

created, Nuwa came down to admire it. The mountains, forests, and rivers were lovely. Still, she felt lonely. She stopped to rest on a riverbank. The clay beneath her felt cool. She began to play with it. First, she molded animals, such as chickens and sheep. When she set them on the ground, they came to life. They pleased her, but they were not good company. She saw her own reflection in the water. She decided to make creatures who looked like her. She sculpted men and women who could talk, dance, and sing. The charming humans cured her loneliness.

2
GODDESSES OF BIRTH AND MOTHERHOOD

Childbirth was a frightening event in ancient times. Many mothers and babies did not survive. Women made offerings and prayed to goddesses of childbirth for help. They hoped these goddesses would ease their birth and protect them and their babies. They also hoped goddesses would watch over their children as they grew up.

GIVING TO THE LIGHT

Ancient Greek women appealed to two goddesses for safe and easy childbirth.

In ancient Greece, mothers often asked goddesses of childbirth for help with labor. They also looked to the goddesses to keep their children safe.

Eileithyia (ee-LEE-thee-uh) was the goddess of childbirth. Her sole purpose was to keep the mother and baby safe from harm. She was the daughter of the goddess Hera and the god Zeus. Artemis was another goddess that Greek women prayed to. Her connection to childbirth begins with her

GODDESSES IN SPACE

Many objects in space are named for goddesses. A dwarf planet in our solar system is called Haumea after a Hawaiian goddess. The planet Venus is named for the Roman goddess of love. People also name space programs after goddesses. For example, NASA has a plan to get people back on the moon. It is called the Artemis program.

own birth. The goddess Leto was expecting twins. The babies' father was Zeus. Hera was jealous of Zeus's love affair with Leto. She threatened to curse any land where Leto gave birth. Leto wandered the earth searching for a place to deliver her babies.

Finally, Leto found the floating island of Delos. Since it wasn't attached to land, Hera's curse would have no effect on Delos. Leto could have her twins there. But Hera wasn't done interfering. She used her powers to hide Leto's labor from Eileithyia. Without the goddess's help, Leto's babies wouldn't come. After nine days, the messenger goddess Iris took pity on Leto. Iris asked Eileithyia to aid Leto. Eileithyia came to Leto's side, and Artemis was born. Artemis then used her divine powers to help her mother. Leto gave birth to the second twin, Apollo.

Mark Greenberg is a scholar of world mythology. He says, "Eileithyia may not be one of the most well-known goddesses today, but in ancient Greece she was prayed to more often than most."[3] Ancient Greeks hoped Eileithyia's help would keep mothers and babies safe.

Mothers in ancient Rome prayed to Juno Lucina. The queen of the Roman gods was also the childbirth goddess.

The Roman goddess of childbirth was Juno, the queen of the Roman gods. When referring to her role in birth, the Romans often called her Juno Lucina. Lucina comes from the Latin word *lucis,* which means

The Hawaiian goddess Haumea made birth safer for mothers. She also eased the pain of childbirth with a special potion.

"light." In Italian, *dare alla luce* means "to give birth" or "to give to the light."

A Hawaiian myth says the goddess Haumea saved women from being doomed to die in childbirth. Long ago, Haumea heard the cries of a chief's daughter. The goddess went to find the cause of the woman's suffering. Haumea found her in pain from labor. The mother-to-be was terrified. The only way that people knew to deliver a baby was to cut it from the mother's body. The mother usually died. Haumea made the woman a potion from a blossom to ease her pain. Then she showed the woman how to push the child from her womb.

RAISING CHILDREN

Mothers in ancient times prayed to goddesses of motherhood to protect their children. In many cultures, the goddess of motherhood was the queen of the gods. This was true of Juno, Hera, and Isis. Another example is Frigg. She is the queen of the Norse goddesses.

Frigg could sometimes see the future. But she never revealed her visions. One day, she saw that her beloved son Balder would soon die. She traveled the world asking everything in creation to promise not to harm him. But she overlooked the mistletoe plant. It was so small and weak that she didn't think it could possibly injure her son. The other gods thought nothing could hurt Balder. They made a game of

The Norse goddess Frigg tried hard to protect her son Balder from harm. But she could not save him from Loki's jealousy.

throwing rocks and spears at him. They admired how Balder was unharmed.

The trickster god Loki was jealous of Balder. He disguised himself as an old woman and went to Frigg. With his clever questions, he learned that the mistletoe had not given its promise. He made a spear tip from its stem. Then he tricked another god into throwing the spear at Balder. It went straight through Balder's heart. He fell dead. This tale shows that mothers can't shield their children from every danger.

Many goddesses of birth and motherhood were also goddesses of farming. Ancient people thought a goddess

FRIGG'S DAY

In English, the sixth day of the week is called Friday. This is a shortened version of "Frigg's day." In Italian, the day is called *venerdi*. This means "day of Venus." Both Frigg and Venus were goddesses of love.

The Slavic goddess Mokosh was believed to help crops grow. Many people asked her for a good harvest.

who could help women raise children could also help people raise crops and herds. One example is the Slavic goddess Mokosh. People left her offerings of fleece and wool. They hoped for a safe pregnancy and easy childbirth in return. They also asked her for rain, a good harvest, and healthy animals.

3
GODDESSES OF DEATH AND THE AFTERLIFE

Many ancient cultures believed in life after death. Some thought the next life would be a paradise. Others thought it would be more like a prison. Many thought it could be either. One's fate was determined by the person's actions in life. Death was the gateway to the afterlife.

In many myths, a goddess rules in the afterlife. Anne Barstow is a retired professor of women's history. She said, "The goddess of death is in reality the goddess of another kind of life."[4]

The Morrigan was said to grant favors to some heroes and kings. But she almost always asked for something in return.

BRINGING DEATH

The Morrigan was a Celtic goddess of death and war. She was really three goddesses in one. She could appear as a beautiful young woman, an old woman, or a crow. The Celts believed that the Morrigan influenced battles by inspiring fear or courage. She also decided which warriors would live and which would die.

The Morrigan once fell in love with a mortal named Cuchulainn (KOO-kul-in). He was a great Irish hero. But Cuchulainn did not return her love. She doomed him to die. One of his enemies heard about the curse

Sometimes the Morrigan appeared as a crow. When this happened, it was a sign of death.

and sent an army to attack Cuchulainn. He faced the enemy force alone. Even Cuchulainn could not win against so many foes. He was wounded by a spear. He tied himself to a boulder so that he could continue to fight. But he died from his wound. Still, the enemy was scared to approach him until the Morrigan landed on his shoulder in the form of a crow. Only then did they believe he was dead. However, Cuchulainn's fate may not have seemed so tragic to the Celts. They believed the afterlife was a paradise where souls waited to be born into a new life.

TRIPLE GODDESSES

The Morrigan is a triple, or triad, goddess. Triad goddesses can be one being who takes three different forms. They may also be three goddesses with a shared purpose. The Greek Fates and Norse Norns are also triad goddesses. They decided people's destiny, including when they would die.

In Norse mythology, Odin sent the Valkyries to battlefields. They decided which souls could go to Valhalla, the afterlife for slain warriors.

The Valkyries (VAL-kuh-reez) of Norse mythology had a lot in common with the Morrigan. They could shape the outcome of battles. The Valkyries also decided who lived and died. They could take the shape of a bird in some stories. But the bird was a swan instead of a crow. The Valkyries were frightful demons in early myths. They were beautiful women in later stories. Also like the Morrigan, some of the Valkyries were involved in sad love stories.

RULING THE DEAD

The Norse believed a paradise awaited fallen warriors. But people who were cowardly or simply died from old age or sickness went to Hel after death. Hel was the name of both a place and the giant goddess who ruled it. Hel was not a place

The fierce goddess Hel ruled over a place of the same name. It was said that she would bring the dead back to fight at the end of the world.

of misery in older stories. But later versions gave grim accounts of Hel. Snorri Sturluson was an Icelandic poet who wrote about

Hel around 1200 CE. He said the goddess Hel was fierce. Sturluson also described the afterlife under Hel's rule. He wrote, "Her hall is called Sleet-Cold; her dish, Hunger; **Famine** is her knife. . . . Disease, her bed."[5] A Norse prophecy said the goddess would bring the dead back to fight at Ragnarok. This was a battle that would bring the end of the old world and the beginning of a new one.

The Greek underworld had an unwilling queen. Persephone (per-SEF-uh-nee) was the daughter of Demeter, the goddess of farming. The god Hades ruled alone

Persephone did not want to marry Hades. He kidnapped her and took her with him to the underworld.

in the underworld. He watched the lovely Persephone from his dark throne. He wanted to marry her. He made a gash in the earth. He then drove his chariot through it and kidnapped her. The Greek poet Homer recorded the story around 700 BCE.

Demeter was heartbroken each time Persephone returned to Hades. The mother's unhappiness was said to be the reason that the weather grew cold.

He spoke of Demeter when Persephone went missing. Homer said, "She vowed that she would never . . . let fruit spring out of the ground, until she beheld with her eyes her own fair-faced daughter."[6]

Zeus feared everyone on earth would starve. He made Hades agree to let Persephone leave the underworld for part of each year. Persephone's return made Demeter happy. She made the weather warm. This allowed crops to grow. The cycle went on as Persephone traveled back and forth. This story explained the seasons to the Greeks.

4

GODDESSES AND GIFTS

Stories of goddesses who gave gifts are part of mythologies from around the world. Gifts could be objects such as tools or weapons. They could also be skills or qualities. Goddesses also gave help, protection, and advice. Some gifts helped a single person. Others benefitted a whole city or nation. Sometimes gifts blessed all the people of the world.

SOLVING PROBLEMS

Ancient China's rivers often flooded. One myth tells of a wise man named Yu who tried to solve this problem. He traveled China for thirteen years showing people

Goddess Peak is a real place that people visit today. The rocks on the northern side look like a beautiful young woman.

how to build canals and **levees**. But when Yu came to the Wushan Mountains, he was stumped. He could find no way to build a canal through the rough peaks.

In one version of the story, Yu got help from the goddess Yao Ji (YOW JEE). She was impressed by Yu's hard work. She used magic to open a passage between

ANCIENT STORIES, MODERN DISASTERS

Floods were important in many Chinese myths. One story about the goddess Nuwa tells how she mended the broken sky to stop a flood. She saved all of humanity. Floods still plague China. As recently as 2021, floods in Henan killed hundreds of people.

the peaks. Thanks to her, the rocks gave way. Yu and his men could dig the canal. The floodwaters flowed out to the sea. Yu became the emperor of China. But Yao Ji was so weary that she had no strength to return to heaven. She stayed in the Wushan Mountains and transformed into Goddess Peak. This peak overlooks the Yangtze River in Eastern China.

GRANTING BOONS

Athena was a popular giver of gifts among the Greeks. She was the goddess of arts, crafts, and war. But she represented courage and strategy rather than anger and violence. Homer described her as “famous among the gods for wisdom.”[7] Long ago, a newly founded Greek city held a contest. The king asked both Athena and Poseidon (puh-SY-duhn) to give the city a gift. The deity who gave the better gift would be **patron** of the city. Poseidon struck the ground with his three-pronged spear. A spring bubbled up through the rocks. But it was salty. The people couldn’t drink the water.

Athena gave the city the first olive tree. The people ate the tasty fruit. They cooked

This olive tree at the Acropolis of Athens is a symbol of Athena. Many people say the goddess herself planted it.

with the olives' oil. They also used the oil to fuel lamps. The tree's wood made strong tools and weapons. Athena won. Many people called the city Athens in her honor. They built her a beautiful temple called the Parthenon.

The Parthenon was built to honor Athena. Many people of Athens still consider the goddess to be their patron.

The Greeks also gave Athena credit for inventing weaving, the plow, and a type of flute called the aulos. Other stories tell of Athena helping mortal heroes. She gave Perseus a bronze shield that helped him defeat the monster Medusa. She gave Bellerophon a magic **bridle**. The bridle let him tame the winged horse Pegasus. Jason had to retrieve a golden fleece to take back his father's kingdom. Athena helped him build the *Argo*, the sturdy ship he used for his quest.

Some of the most treasured gifts goddesses gave people were stories. Myths of goddesses have entertained people for thousands of years. These stories also offer

A POPULAR GODDESS

Americans have long admired Athena. In 1897, the city of Nashville, Tennessee, built an exact copy of the Parthenon. In 1990, they added a 42-foot (12.8 m) statue of the goddess. Many movies, television shows, books, and video games feature Athena too.

Athena's gift to Bellerophon helped him defeat a fierce monster called Chimera. By riding Pegasus, the hero was able to wound the monster from above.

hope. Because of these stories, people believed goddesses would help and protect them and their loved ones. Goddess myths inspire people with examples of courage, strength, and wisdom. Many of these myths are still told today. Joseph Campbell

GODDESSES OF WORLD MYTHOLOGY

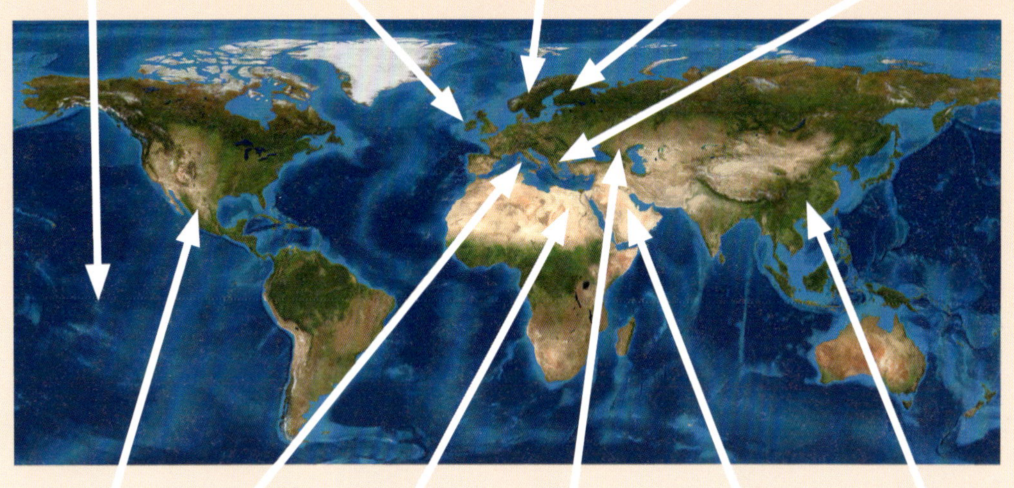

Each ancient culture had its own set of goddesses and myths that told the goddesses' stories.

was a scholar who studied mythology. He thought the goddesses of the past would help to shape "the possibilities of the feminine future."[8]

GLOSSARY

bridle

a set of straps that encircles a horse's head and allows the horse to be directed

chaos

disorder and confusion

deities

gods and goddesses

famine

a severe lack of food for a large number of people

incense

spices or other materials that make a pleasant smell when burned

levees

ridges or walls, usually made of dirt, that hold back water

patron

a person or god who supports and helps a group or cause; in return, the group honors its patron

SOURCE NOTES

CHAPTER ONE: GODDESSES OF CREATION

1. Elias Lönnrot, J.M. Crawford, trans., "Kalevala," *The Public Domain Review*, 1898. https://publicdomainreview.org.

2. Plutarch, Frank Cole Babbitt, trans., "Moralia," *Loeb Classical Library*, 1936. http://penelope.uchicago.edu.

CHAPTER TWO: GODDESSES OF BIRTH AND MOTHERHOOD

3. Mark Greenberg, "Eileithyia: The Greek Goddess of Childbirth," *Mythology Source*, February 22, 2021. https://mythologysource.com.

CHAPTER THREE: GODDESSES OF DEATH AND THE AFTERLIFE

4. Anne Barstow, "The Uses of Archeology for Women's History: James Mellaart's Work on the Neolithic Goddess at Çatal Hüyük," *Feminist Studies*, October 1978, pp. 7–18.

5. Martha Anne and Dorothy Myers Imel, *Goddesses in World Mythology*. Santa Barbara, CA: ABC-CLIO, 1993, p. 84.

6. Homer, H.G. Evelyn-White, trans., *Homeric Hymns*. New York: The Macmillan Co., 1920, p. 313.

CHAPTER FOUR: GODDESSES AND GIFTS

7. Homer, Robert Fagles, trans., *The Odyssey*. New York: Penguin Books, 1996, p. 296.

8. Thomas Apel, "Hel (Realm)." *Mythopedia*, November 20, 2021. https://mythopedia.com.

FOR FURTHER RESEARCH

BOOKS

Xanthe Gresham-Knight, *Goddesses and Heroines: Women of Myth and Legend*. New York: Thames & Hudson, Inc., 2020.

Marchella Ward, *Gods of the Ancient World: A Kids' Guide to Ancient Mythologies, From Mayan to Norse, Egyptian to Yoruba*. New York: DK Children, 2022.

Pam Watts, *Gods of World Mythology*. San Diego, CA: BrightPoint Press, 2023.

INTERNET SOURCES

"Five Greek Goddesses of Mt. Olympus Who Helped Rule the World," *Kids News*, May 14, 2019. www.kidsnews.com.

"The Gods and Goddesses of Ancient Greece!" *National Geographic Kids*, n.d. www.natgeokids.com.

"Viking Gods," *DK Find Out!*, 2022. www.dkfindout.com.

WEBSITES

Discovering Ancient Egypt
https://discoveringegypt.com

This site features information about many Egyptian gods and goddesses. Activities, videos, articles, and more are included.

Greek Mythology
www.greekmythology.com

This source has dozens of articles on Greek gods, goddesses, and heroes. It also includes a few articles on related Roman and Norse myths.

Mythopedia
https://mythopedia.com

This site offers more than 200 articles about mythology from nine different cultures. It aims to educate and entertain readers with its content.

INDEX

IMAGE CREDITS

Cover: © Corey Ford/Alamy
5: © Rudall 30/Shutterstock Images
7: © Funtay/Shutterstock Images
8: © Local Doctor/Shutterstock Images
10: © Hoika Mikhail/Shutterstock Images
13: © Fine Art Images/Heritage Images Partnership Ltd/Alamy
16: © John Mitchell/Alamy
18: © Akimov Konstantin/Shutterstock Images
22: © Pictures From History/CPA Media PTE Ltd/Alamy
25: © Gilmanshin/Shutterstock Images
30: © Global Moments/iStockphoto
33: © Claudine VM/iStockphoto
35: © Flip Foto/iStockphoto
29: © J. Photos/Shutterstock Images
37: © Maunka/iStockphoto
39: © Andrea Ghelfi/Shutterstock Images
41: © Warm Tail/Shutterstock Images
43: © Creativica Xeravin/Shutterstock Images
45: © Delcarmat/Shutterstock Images
46: © IMG Stock Photo/Shutterstock Images
49: © HSDC/Shutterstock Images
53: © By Valet/Shutterstock Images
54: © Preto Perola/Shutterstock Images
56: © Insima/Shutterstock Images
57: © Viacheslav Lopatin/Shutterstock Images

ABOUT THE AUTHOR

Rachel Bithell writes fiction and nonfiction for children and their caregivers. A former physicist and teacher, she has particular enthusiasm for STEM and history. She lives in Colorado with her family, which was grown through birth, foster care, and adoption. Her writing has appeared in several national magazines. This is her second book for young people.